THIS WALKER BOOK BELONGS TO:

Louise

with best wishes

Sue
Heap.

To Ann Barr and
Gina and Murray Pollinger
P.B.

To Anna, Matthew
and Jack
S.H.

and with thanks to
Michael Reynolds of the
World Parrot Trust
for his help and advice.

If you ever adopt a parrot, please MAKE SURE it isn't one that has been captured in the wild and imported. The international trade in wild birds is very cruel, and a bird that has been used to flying freely in a forest will never adjust to life with you. Make sure the parrot is one – like Turkey – that has been hatched and reared in captivity, in the country where you get it, and remember that you will have to devote a lot of time to its care, perhaps for the rest of your life.

First published 1994
by Walker Books Ltd
87 Vauxhall Walk
London SE11 5HJ

This edition published 1996

10 9 8 7 6 5 4 3 2 1

This book has been typeset in ITC Garamond Light.

Printed in Hong Kong

British Library Cataloguing in Publication Data
A catalogue record for this book is available
from the British Library.

ISBN 0-7445-4727-X

TOWN PARROT

Written by Penelope Bennett

Illustrated by Sue Heap

WALKER BOOKS

AND SUBSIDIARIES

LONDON · BOSTON · SYDNEY

This is a parrot's eye,
the eye of a parrot called Turkey.

Turkey is a Blue-fronted
Amazon parrot.
The feathers on her head
and body are small, soft
and rounded. Her tail and
wing feathers are long and
strong for flying.

She was hatched in an aviary,
six or seven years ago.

This is how she looked
when she was 7 days old...

15 days old...

26 days old...

6 months old...
Turkey could live
until she's 50 years old.

9

She should be living
in a tree in the
Amazon forest,
with a parrot family.
But she isn't.

She lives on the
top floor of a house
in town with a
writer called Ann.

Considering Ann's a human being,
Turkey gets on very well with her.

Ann works at home,
so she spends a lot of
time with Turkey.
This is what parrots
who live with people need.

Every day Turkey wakes up at about
half past eight and shouts, "Hello, Turkey!"
in a rather hoarse voice.

While Ann has her bath, Turkey grooms her feathers with her beak. Then she flies to the window and looks down at the people in the street below, whistling and calling to them.

A parrot's lower beak looks square from the front, like a chisel. The upper beak has ridges underneath, like a file.
The tongue is strong, round and black.

When Ann goes into the kitchen to make breakfast, Turkey rushes in too – her feet pit-pattering on the floorboards. She perches on Ann's shoulder and nibbles her ear.
If she's stirring porridge, Turkey waddles sideways down her arm and takes the spoon.

If she's eating muesli, Turkey stands on her lap and picks out the nuts and raisins. When she finds a whole nut she takes it between her toes and turns it round and round.

Parrots are the only birds who can feed themselves with their feet. With her feet, Turkey can waddle, climb, hold, cling, clasp, unpack and pull.

After breakfast she has a snooze, her beak tucked into her feathers, her eyes half open, always alert.

As soon as she hears the postman she flies to the hall and watches the letters landing on the mat. Quite often she attacks them.

Parrots need to be busy.
In the forest, they're flying,
climbing, peeling bark,
chattering and cracking nuts.
When they live with people who
neglect them, they become sad,
bored and silent.

When Turkey wants to play she nips Ann on the hand. If Ann's not in the room to play with her, she likes taking the spines off the backs of books.

She also likes sorting through cupboards and drawers, tossing things out. Her favourite cupboard was the hat cupboard, until Ann put the hats in boxes. Now she likes the kitchen cupboard best.

Sometimes Ann finds Turkey hanging upside down in the hall.

When the telephone rings she attacks it. Last time it went wrong the telephone engineer said, "*Someone*'s been meddling with it." *Someone* sat swinging innocently on her perch.

Turkey has also removed the control knobs from several plastic clocks and uses them to play football.

Town parrots need people to keep them out of danger.
Wires can be dangerous!

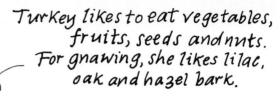

Turkey likes to eat vegetables, fruits, seeds and nuts. For gnawing, she likes lilac, oak and hazel bark.

Usually Ann and Turkey have lunch together.
Afterwards Turkey has a nap on Ann's bed.

20

Wild parrots nest in hollow trees. Perhaps under-the-bed feels like a hollow.

Or she squeezes underneath it, and talks to herself in a strange little mewing voice.

In the afternoon she helps Ann with her window box. She pulls out the sticks Ann's just put in.

Once a week Ann gives her a shower in the bathroom, then dries her gently with a hair dryer. Turkey does her voice exercises in the bathroom, too, because that's the room where her voice sounds best. Ann used to think that she wanted her to listen, but she doesn't. She stops as soon as Ann comes into the room. But when *Ann* wants to listen to music, Turkey insists on joining in, piping and fluting. Sometimes they have whistling duets.

Parrots need showers. In the forest they rain-bathe in the tree tops.

After dinner, Turkey watches
television. She quite likes the news,
but not the nature programmes.

When sparrows come to Ann's bird table, Turkey
ignores them. But she never ignores cats or dogs,
however big they are. She tries to be friendly by
stretching out her foot to them.

When she stretches out *her* foot to Ann, it means that she wants to be picked up.

When Ann and Turkey go away by train for the weekend, Turkey travels free in the guard's van, with the bicycles.

She also enjoys driving in the car. She looks out of the window and purrs.

Ann sometimes takes her to parties, where she's often the most interesting guest. When Ann dances, Turkey sways backwards and forwards on her shoulder screeching with pleasure.

When it's time to go to bed, Turkey follows Ann into the bathroom and watches her washing.

Then she wants to be taken to her cage, and gets cross if she has to wait.

Once she's inside and her cage is covered, she's ready to go to sleep … until the next day arrives.

Look up the pages
to find out about all
these parrot things.
Don't forget to look
at both kinds of
words: this kind
and *this kind*.